FTB

D0096436

Parents and Caregivers,

Stone Arch Readers are designed to provide enjoyable reading experiences, as well as opportunities to develop vocabulary, literacy skills, and comprehension. Here are a few ways to support your beginning reader:

- Talk with your child about the ideas addressed in the story.

- Discuss each illustration, mentioning the characters, where they are, and what they are doing.

- Read with expression, pointing to each word. You may want to read the whole story through and then revisit parts of the story to ensure that the meanings of words or phrases are understood.

- Talk about why the character did what he or she did and what your child would do in that situation.

- Help your child connect with characters and events in the story.

Remember, reading with your child should be fun, not forced. Each moment spent reading with your child is a priceless investment in his or her literacy life.

Gail Saunders-Smith, Ph.D.

STONE ARCH **READERS**

are published by Stone Arch Books
A Capstone Imprint
151 Good Counsel Drive, P.O. Box 669
Mankato, Minnesota 56002
www.capstonepub.com

Copyright © 2010 by Stone Arch Books
All rights reserved. No part of this publication may be reproduced
in whole or in part, or stored in a retrieval system, or transmitted in any
form or by any means, electronic, mechanical, photocopying, recording,
or otherwise, without written permission of the publisher.
Printed in the United States of America in Melrose Park, Illinois.
122010
006029R

Library of Congress Cataloging-in-Publication Data
Crow, Melinda Melton.
Tired trucks / by Melinda Melton Crow ; illustrated by Patrick Girouard.
p. cm. — (Stone Arch readers)
ISBN 978-1-4342-1864-3 (library binding)
ISBN 978-1-4342-2299-2 (pbk.)
[1. Trucks—Fiction.] I. Girouard, Patrick, ill. II. Title.
PZ7.C88536Dr 2010
[E]—dc22

                                            2009034207

Summary: Three truck buddies work hard on the farm.

Art Director: Kay Fraser
Graphic Designer: Hilary Wacholz
Production Specialist: Michelle Biedscheid

Reading Consultants:
Gail Saunders-Smith, Ph.D.
Melinda Melton Crow, M.Ed.
Laurie K. Holland, Media Specialist

THE MISSING MOUSE

Every time you turn the page,
look for the little mouse.

E CRO
1676 9518   12-14-12   FTB
Crow, Melinda Melton.

Tired trucks

          SDW

TIRED TRUCKS

by Melinda Melton Crow

illustrated by Patrick Girouard

LeRoy Collins Leon County
PUBLIC LIBRARY SYSTEM
200 West Park Avenue
Tallahassee, Florida 32301-7720

STONE ARCH BOOKS
a capstone imprint

This is Green Truck.
This is Yellow Truck.
This is Blue Truck.

The trucks work all day.
They are tired.

The trucks take a nap.
Then they go back to work.

"Where is Yellow Truck?"
asks Blue Truck.

Green Truck goes to look for
Yellow Truck.

Blue Truck goes to look for
Yellow Truck, too.

Yellow Truck is still sleeping.

"Wake up, Yellow Truck," says
Green Truck.

"I am up! I am up!" says
Yellow Truck.

Green Truck goes back to work.

Yellow Truck goes to work, too.

Blue Truck is not there.

Now the trucks have to look
for Blue Truck.

Blue Truck is sleeping.
"We are tired trucks," says
Green Truck.

STORY WORDS

work   nap   wake

tired   sleeping

Total Word Count: 113

Follow your favorite **TRUCK** pals as they **learn** about the **open road.**

STONE ARCH **READERS**   LEVEL 1

DRIVE ALONG

by Melinda Melton Crow

STONE ARCH **READERS**   LEVEL 1

LITTLE WHEELS

by Melinda Melton Crow

STONE ARCH **READERS**   LEVEL 1

MUD MESS

by Melinda Melton Crow

STONE ARCH **READERS**   LEVEL 1

RIDE AND SEEK

by Melinda Melton Crow